To our dad, Charles Honaker, who never took a trip without Traveling Tootsie hiding in a shoe in his suitcase, and to our mom, Peggy, who always helped us find the perfect hiding spot.

MASCOT KIDS!

an imprint of Amplify Publishing Group

www.mascotbooks.com

Traveling Tootsie

For more information, please contact:
Mascot Books, an imprint of Amplify Publishing Group
620 Herndon Parkway, Suite 320
Herndon, VA 20170
info@mascotbooks.com

Library of Congress Control Number: 2021924934

CPSIA Code: PRT0522A

ISBN-13: 978-1-64543-588-4

Printed in the United States

TRAVELING TOOTSIE

KAREN & KATHY HONAKER
ILLUSTRATED BY CHIARA CIVATI

Katie and Steven are upset. They want to go with Daddy on his work trip to Washington, DC. Why do they always have to stay home? Why do Mommy and Daddy always get to have all the fun? They wished they could hide in Daddy's suitcase and sneak out for one of their own adventures!

Katie and Steven decide to head to the playroom and pretend they are going on a trip too. They set up little chairs and strap their stuffed animals in their seatbelts so they can get ready to take off on the airplane! Their favorite little yellow teddy bear gets to be the pilot. Katie and Steven say, "If we can't go with Daddy, then we'll go on our very own journey!"

Katie and Steven realized that they can't get on a plane without luggage, so they start packing their bags with the most important items they can find!

After running all around their room, Steven, slightly out of breath, yells, "I wish we could ride in Daddy's suitcase and go with him!"

While Katie paused to think about their dilemma, she said, "That's going to make Daddy's suitcase way too heavy!"

Suddenly, Pilot Teddy said, "I know what we can do! Hide me in Daddy's suitcase, and I'll go and see Washington, DC! Then I can come home and tell you all about it!"

Katie and Steven gasp, and look at each other with wide eyes. They had never heard their teddy talk before—let alone suggest such an exciting idea! They started jumping up and down with excitement and shouting in unison, "Let's do it!"

The night before the big trip, Katie and Steven were so excited that they barely slept!

In the morning, they sneak into their parents' bedroom and find Daddy's suitcase still open on the bed. They decide to hide their teddy bear deep down in one of Daddy's big shoes so no one will see him. They whisper goodbye, wish him good luck, and remind him to make sure he comes back with lots of stories to share!

Steven looks at Katie and says, "Since he's in Daddy's shoe where your toes go, we should call him Tootsie!"

Tootsie couldn't wait to head out on an exciting adventure like this one! He'd never been on a plane before!

Tootsie got settled inside Daddy's shoe, and he took a long nap while on the airplane ride. He needed his rest so that he would be ready to explore when he got to Washington, DC. He barely even felt the turbulence as the plane shook in the sky.

Tootsie waited until Daddy left the hotel room every morning, and then he snuck out to go on his own adventure. Tootsie saw so many things in Washington, DC...

He went to see the White House where the President of the United States lives, and he passed Nationals Park, where he could smell the hot dogs at the ballpark and hear all the baseball fans cheering.

This was a lot of walking, so Tootsie decided to hop on a bus tour so he could see as much of the city as he could without getting too tired.

He saw the US Capitol where laws are made, and he rode past the wharf and could smell all the fish at the market.

When the bus stopped at the National Zoo, he hopped off to stroll through and see all the animals—his favorites were the pandas!

He visited the Smithsonian Museums, which are filled with spaceships, airplanes, dinosaurs, paintings, and even a Teddy Bear—just like Tootsie!

He didn't know if he could make it, but Tootsie even climbed the 897 steps to reach the top of the Washington Monument!

Next, Tootsie headed down to the Tidal Basin and rented a paddle boat. He paddled past the Jefferson and Martin Luther King, Jr. Memorials, then followed the currents of the Potomac River.

He headed toward Georgetown and could hear music coming from the Kennedy Center and the bells ringing at

the National Cathedral. He was exhausted when he finally
made it back!

Tootsie made it back to the hotel just in time to hide before Daddy returned and started packing his suitcase so that he could head back home. Tootsie crawled back into Daddy's shoe, settled in, and was ready for a good long nap on the plane ride home. The next morning, Katie and Steven rushed to find their daddy's suitcase. They got Tootsie out of Daddy's big shoe and ran into the playroom. Tootsie told them all about Washington, DC, and the exciting adventure he had there!

When Katie asked what Tootsie's favorite part was, Tootsie got a dreamy look on his face and answered, "The smell of the cherry blossoms."

Katie and Steven looked at each other and hoped that one day, they would get to smell them, too.

After all of the storytelling, Katie exclaimed, "I think your new name should be 'Traveling Tootsie'!"

Steven and Tootsie loved the idea, and from then on, the children called him "Traveling Tootsie." They also realized that since Traveling Tootsie fits so well inside Daddy's shoe, he can go on all of his and Mommy's trips too. Steven and Katie wouldn't be sad about Mommy or Daddy leaving anymore!

That night they all snuggled up in their beds, and Traveling Tootsie dreamed of where he would go next...

aBOUT THE aUTHORS

Kathy and Karen grew up in the Chicago suburbs
and moved to Virginia as teenagers. They enjoyed
many family vacations, which began their love of
travel. They both reside in Virginia with their families
and continue to instill a love of travel with their own
children. This is their first children's book written
together, about a favorite childhood memory that
they always wanted to share with others to enjoy.
They hope to inspire a sense of adventure in you!